The Principal Who Made SCHOOL the Best Part of Each Student's Day

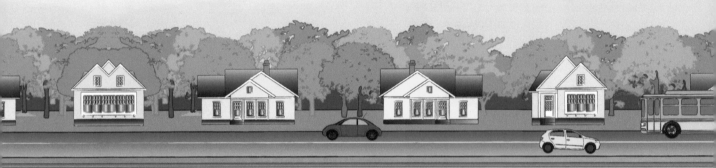

PALMETTO
PUBLISHING

Charleston, SC

www.PalmettoPublishing.com

The Principal Who Made School the Best Part of Each Student's Day

Copyright © 2020 by Joyce Stewart

ISBN-13: 978-1-64111-853-8

ISBN-10: 1-64111-853-9

The Principal Who Made SCHOOL the Best Part of Each Student's Day

Dr. Joyce Stewart

To my adopted daughters' Korean birth mothers for giving me my life's greatest gifts, Jodi and Jill.

To Mary W for showing so many of us what happens to a piece of writing by simply changing one word.

To Erin, publishing consultant from Palmetto Publishing, for providing meaningful and timely feedback.

To school and district leaders who have the courage to make decisions and lead in the service of students and their families.

And most of all, to teachers who intentionally PLAN and engage students in learning that makes their brains sweat.

My mother died of cancer one month before I started middle school. I remember her curly hair, infectious laugh, and the way she made each moment extraordinary. There are no words to explain the pain and hopelessness I experienced. I tried everything to keep my mother alive, and in the end, all I could give her was a promise. I promised her I would work to find a cure for cancer.

I could not imagine starting or ending my school days without my mom. My dad and I did our very best to prepare for the start of a new school year. Getting a new backpack, supplies, and clothes and attending the before-school orientation were the easy parts. But getting out of bed...was difficult until I met Ms. Fiona, my new principal.

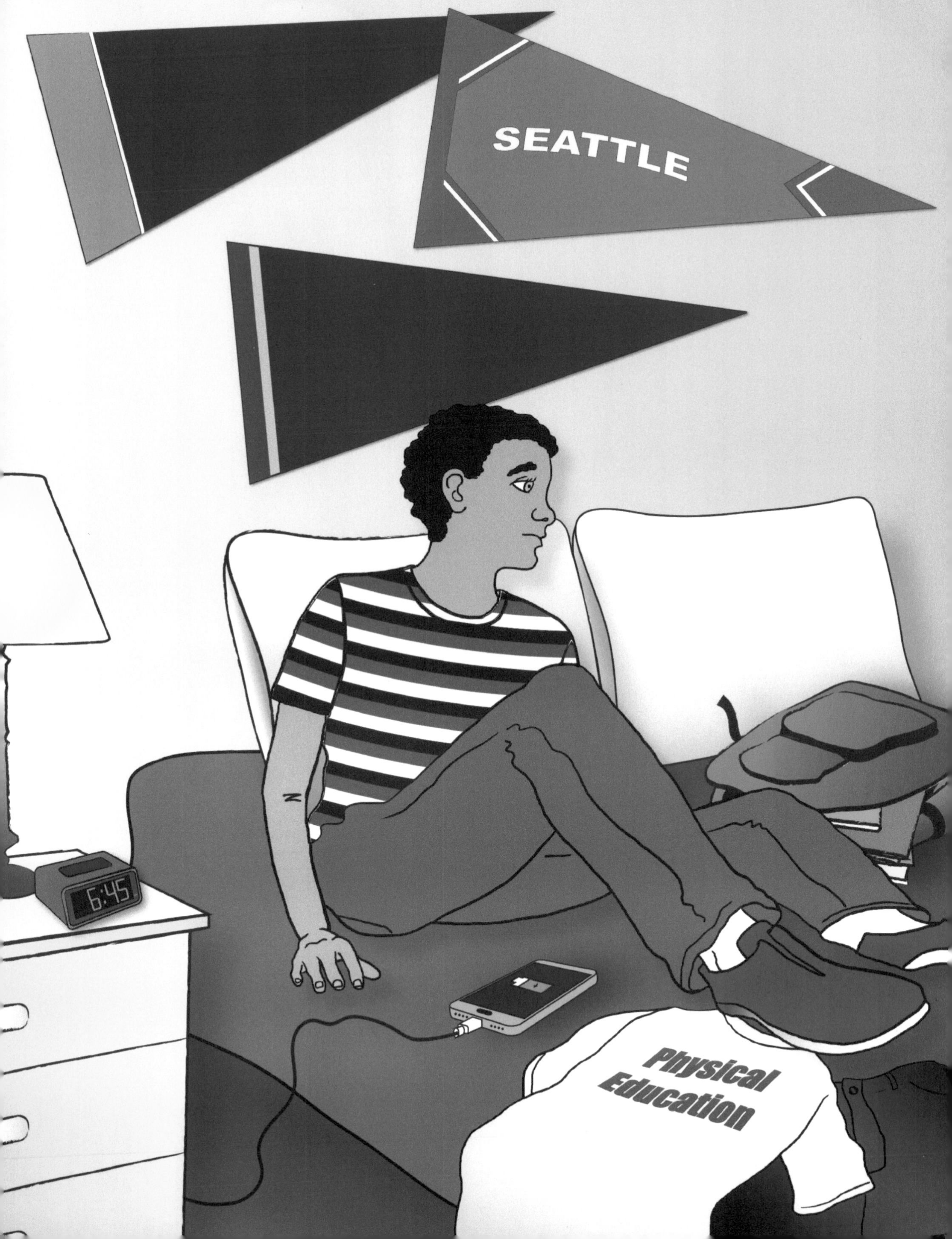
SEATTLE
6:45
Physical
Education

It was the first day of school, and my dad dropped me off at school on his way to work. He worked at a company that allowed employees to bring their dogs to work, so Winston, our family dog, was with us each morning. Over one thousand students attended my middle school, and the car drop-off lane was so long. Parents did not seem to mind waiting in line because they knew they would be greeted by Ms. Fiona.

As the year progressed, the seasons changed. Sun, rain, or snow, Ms. Fiona was always out in the drop-off lane in one of her many stylish outfits that often included heels or boots.

She opened our car door and said, "Good morning, Bodie, Mr. Rowan, and Winston. I am so excited to see you today. Make each moment count today. Plan to attend *The Lion King*, our drama performance, this weekend. Remember, Bodie, we need you to find a cure for cancer."

I know our principal is the only principal who greets each student each morning. No meeting or email was more important than greeting students, their family members, and even the animals. And even though my heart was still hurting from the loss of my mother, that greeting helped me jump out of bed in the morning.

After she left the car drop-off area, I saw Ms. Fiona dashing to the bus loading and unloading area and greeting students as they got off buses. Students stopped to tell her important news in their lives. Then she quickly headed to the cafeteria to make sure students got breakfast. Finally, I heard her heels as she walked with purpose and smile through each hall and greeted teachers who were out in the halls welcoming students, saying, "Make students' brains sweat today." No meeting or email was more important than greeting teachers before the school day started. And I know that little act of kindness made teachers want to work for Ms. Fiona.

Ms. Fiona visited classrooms each day. Our teachers made sure they had learning targets posted, and each student understood what they had to do to reach the target. When Ms. Fiona visited my classrooms, she took the time to look at students' work. I especially liked it when she looked at my science journal. She said, "Bodie, you are on your way to discovering a cure for cancer."

I know our principal is the only principal who knows the goals and aspirations of each of her students. Her comments helped me jump out of bed in the morning.

My teachers liked when Ms. Fiona visited classrooms because she always posted a *little* note on their desks or to their computer screens. My teachers hung the notes on their bulletin boards behind their desks.

One day I read a note from Ms. Fiona to Ms. Jill, my science teacher. It said, "From the desk of Ms. Fiona. Thank you, Ms. Jill, for attending the students' music concert last night. Thank you also for writing descriptive feedback in your students' science journals."

I know our principal is the only principal who visits students' classrooms each day, interacts with the students, and leaves hope-filled notes for our teachers. Those notes made my teachers smile, and those smiles were contagious to students.

By lunchtime, I was starving and really missed the lunches my mom used to pack. But I was so surprised when I discovered that our school cook made the best hot lunches with so many choices! No wonder so many students ordered hot lunch. We also had "communities of student interest" in our school. Sometimes during our lunchtime, I attended the grief counseling session. Ms. Fiona stood at the lunchroom door and greeted each student by name as they walked in. Students complimented her on her *cool* outfits. As students ate, Ms. Fiona walked around the cafeteria talking to them. She knew each student's grades too. Many times she asked, "Is anyone being bullied?" Ms. Fiona did not tolerate bullying; she wanted everyone to feel safe. If students were disrespectful, they had to attend Ms. Fiona's Friday after-school reteaching classes until they could be respectful with others. I know our principal is the only principal who cares so much about bullying because she stays late on Fridays to help students understand the impact of bullying or help them make up missing assignments.

Ms. Fiona's office had a big window. I liked looking into it because she always had fresh flowers on her desk and pictures of her daughters on her bulletin board. It reminded me of my mom because she always had fresh flowers on our kitchen table and pictures of my dad and me all over the house. Ms. Fiona's desk was very organized, and I wondered when she got her work completed because I never saw her sitting by her computer during the school day. She always carried a walkie-talkie and did a lot of face-to-face adult talk in the hall as she moved through the building. Her visibility everywhere helped create a sense of calm and confidence with teachers, students, and their parents.

I know our principal is the only principal who takes time to smell the flowers, and those fresh flowers made my heart feel better.

I could not wait to go to our P.E. and health class because the teachers chose me to lead the daily warm-ups. Ms. Fiona would stop by and join us in the warm-ups. Even with her dress and heels on, she could hold her planks longer than any student, do as many jumping jacks, and motivate students to keep up with her. She modeled that our physical education/health class was the most important class in the school because if we did not take care of ourselves, nothing else mattered.

I know our principal is the only principal who joined the physical education classes and did planks and jumping jacks in a dress and high heels.

Each Wednesday afternoon, Ms. Fiona made a positive end-of-the day announcement before school ended. Then she reminded us to quickly clear campus so teachers could start their "collaborative team" meetings in 10 minutes.

I never knew what "collaborative team" meetings meant, but teachers hustled to their meeting rooms, and students cleared campus. When Ms. Fiona said she *needed* us to do something, we all did it.

I know our principal is the only principal who knows what is possible when all adults in the building share their gifts, talents, and experiences on a team.

Rain, snow, or shine, Ms. Fiona was always at the car or bus lines during dismissal. All meetings waited until students were on our way home. She told us to make sure we read that evening. Because she knew our interests, she would order us our favorite authors and give us books as we got on the bus or in our car. She found me several titles about the cure for cancer and how to deal with grief.

I know our principal is the only principal who takes the time to connect students to books that match their interests.

When I got into the car one afternoon, my dad told me he received a positive phone call from Ms. Fiona. She told him about the work in my science journal. She said I deserved my favorite dinner! My dad went to the grocery store and got the ingredients for homemade chicken noodle soup.

I know our principal is the only principal who calls each student's parent before the end of the year and shares a positive message.

That evening, the sixth grade class had a band concert directed by Mr. Jodi, our band teacher. We enjoyed my favorite meal and hurried to the concert. I was excited because Mr. Jodi said I could play a solo in honor of my mother. Ms. Fiona was standing at the entrance to the auditorium, greeting parents, and handing them a program. Before the concert started, she took the microphone and told parents about all the celebrations at our middle school. She also shared the challenges and how parents and grandparents could help.

I know our principal is the only principal who greets each parent and student at the door and brags about the school before a performance begins.

Every spring, Ms. Fiona made sure each grade level had a career fair, and students rotated through the careers. Each student filled out a questionnaire to show what they learned from the speaker.

Before the fair, Ms. Fiona had student focus groups and gathered input. I appreciated that she listened to my interests and invited a cancer researcher from Fred Hutchinson Cancer Research Center in Seattle. That was the job I wanted when I graduated from college.

The summer before I started seventh grade, I was worried about how I was going to get through my first summer without my mom. I would be home alone a lot. That summer Ms. Fiona invited me to be a teacher's assistant at my old elementary school. She said the principal specifically requested me!

In my district, elementary students needing extra help and support attend summer school. As a summer teacher's assistant, I helped those students solve difficult math problems. Kids loved the way I made learning fun. I could not wait to get up on each summer morning!

Before I entered high school, Ms. Fiona met with the high school principal, my dad, and me. She shared my life's goals and aspirations. She knew each student because since sixth grade, she had been meeting with a support team once a month and looking at each student's academic and social-emotional data.

The principal helped my dad and me map out a schedule that would prepare me for my future.

Other parents and students sat in chairs outside the high school principal's office to meet with Ms. Fiona and him.

I know Ms. Fiona is the only principal who meets with the high school principal, students, and their parents to personalize schedules. She took great pride in checking in with the high school principal on how the students were doing. With her ongoing support and encouragement, I was able to get good grades throughout high school.

After graduating from high school, I attended my mom's alma mater, a small private college in Montana. My excellent grades, community service, and activities allowed me to secure a scholarship at Carroll College. The college had an excellent premed program, and after I graduated, I was accepted to medical school.

My dad and I surprised Ms. Fiona and my middle and high school teachers by sending them an invitation to attend my graduation from medical school.

I spent the next eight years studying to be an oncologist, a doctor who treats cancer and provides medical care for people diagnosed with cancer. I treat each of my patients like I would want my mom to be treated. In honor of my mom, I also work closely with cancer researchers at Fred Hutchinson Cancer Research Center and share my experiences and insights.

I will never give up on finding
a cure for cancer, and I get
to do that important work
because I had a middle
school principal who created
a culture of calm during a
difficult time in my life and
made school the
best part of my day!

Dr. Stewart can be contacted at
joycmstewart@gmail.com.

CPSIA information can be obtained
at www.ICGtesting.com
Printed in the USA
LVHW072132200121
676967LV00004B/118

* 9 7 8 1 6 4 1 1 1 8 5 3 8 *